maybe we will stop at a motel with a pool

3 FT

Pictures from Our vacation

Lynne Rae Perkins

a·a·a·y·y·i·i·i·e·e·e·e

GREENWILLOW BOOKS, An Imprint of HarperCollins

Pen and ink and watercolor paint were used to prepare the full-color art. The text type is Cochin. Library of Congress Cataloging-in-Publication Data
Perkins, Lynne Rae. Pictures from our vacation / by Lynne Rae Perkins. p. cm. "Greenwillow Books." Summary: Given a camera that takes and prints tiny pictures just before leaving for the family farm, a young girl records a vacation that gets off to a slow start, but winds up being a family reunion filled with good memories. ISBN-13: 978-0-06-085097-5 (trade bdg.) ISBN-10; 0-06-085097-3 (trade bdg.) ISBN-13: 978-0-06-085098-2 (lib. bdg.) ISBN-10: 0-06-085098-1 (lib. bdg.) [1. Vacations—Fiction. 2. Family reunions—Fiction. 3. Photography—Fiction.] 1. Title.
PZ7.P4313 Pic 2007 [E]—22 2006049256   Greenwillow Books   First Edition 10 9 8 7 6 5 4 3 2 1

for the Davidsons (is Aunt Nostalgia here yet?)

Just before we got in the car to go on our vacation, our mother said, "Oh, I almost forgot!" From her bag she pulled out a little camera for me, and one for my brother.

The cameras took tiny pictures that shot out right away. We could watch the pictures appear, then peel off the backs and stick them on something.

Our mom gave us notebooks to stick them in.

"They will be souvenirs of our vacation," she said.

I TOOK MY
First Picture
BY Mistake.

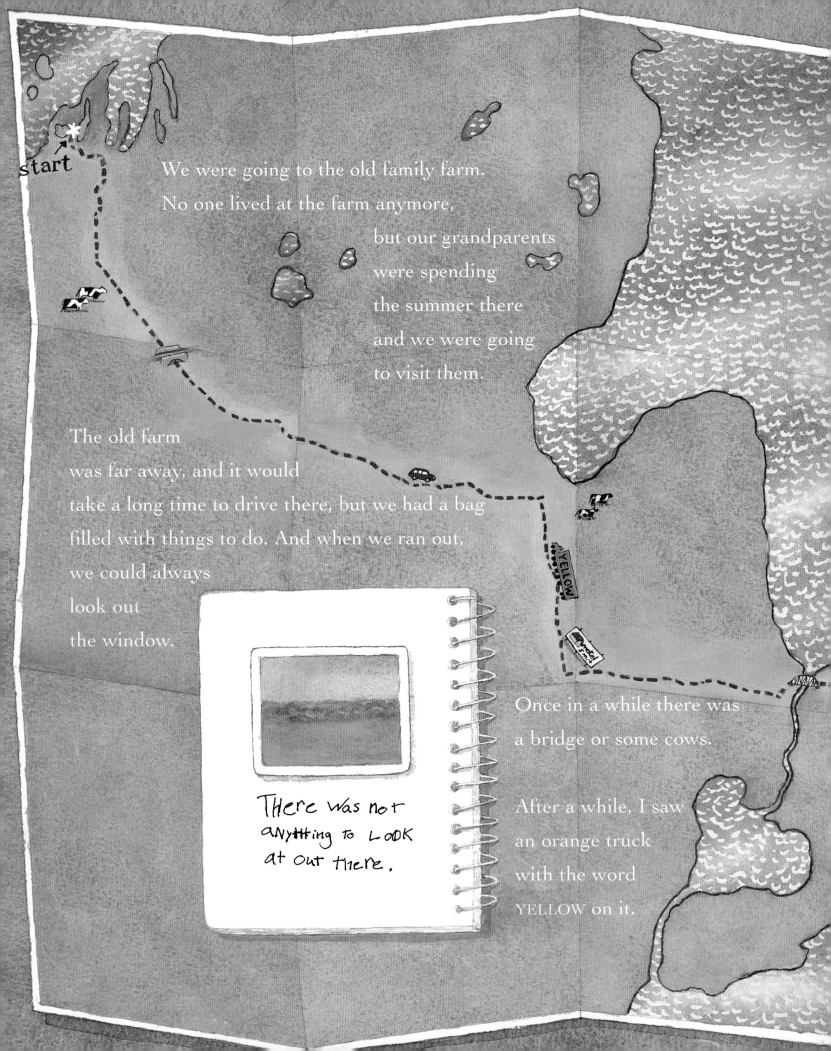

start

We were going to the old family farm.
No one lived at the farm anymore,
but our grandparents
were spending
the summer there
and we were going
to visit them.

The old farm
was far away, and it would
take a long time to drive there, but we had a bag
filled with things to do. And when we ran out,
we could always
look out
the window.

There was not anything to LOOK at Out there.

Once in a while there was
a bridge or some cows.

After a while, I saw
an orange truck
with the word
YELLOW on it.

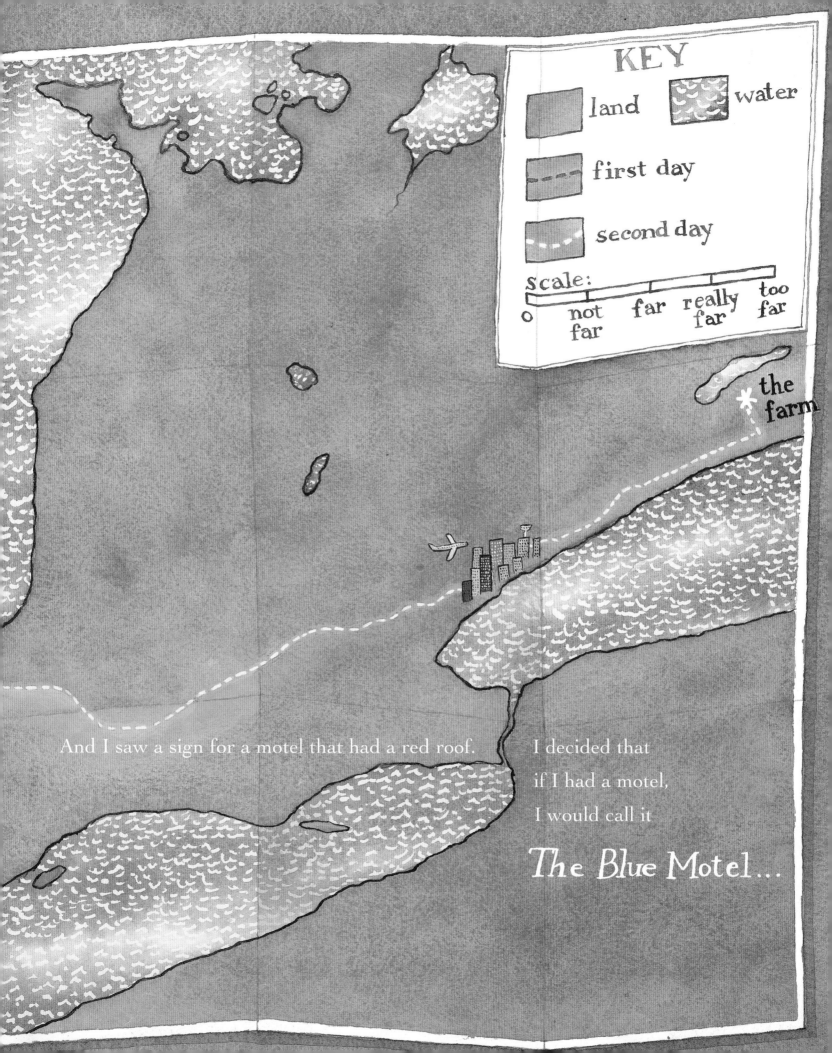

And I saw a sign for a motel that had a red roof. I decided that if I had a motel, I would call it

The Blue Motel...

It would be the kind of motel that has separate cottages. On the outside, they would all be blue, but inside, each one would be different.

The Jungle Cottage would have hammocks. The shower would be a waterfall.

There would be a cottage where a whole wall would be an aquarium, with real fish.

Maybe it would have sand on the floor, and buckets and shovels.

At night, you could build a bonfire, but just a small one.

There would be a Sun Cottage.
The bed would glow like the sun
but you could turn it off at night.

Maybe the lampshades would
have clouds on them that would
spin around the sun — sometimes
slow, sometimes fast.

There would be heat in the carpet.

You would need to
wear sunblock in there.

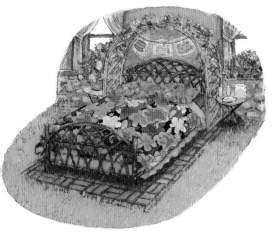

The Flower Garden Cottage
would have real grass.

There would be a Moon Cottage,
all silvery and deep blue.

And a Star Cottage.

People would be so surprised when they
opened the door and went inside.

By the time I stopped thinking about
The Blue Motel, it was dark and we were
looking for a real motel.

The real motel was called the Shangri-La.
The sign said it had a POOL.

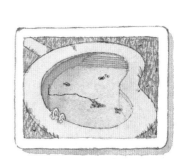

There was a
Pool but it didn't
have water in it.

The second day was almost exactly the same as the first day except that for lunch, we stopped at a place where you could get gravy on your french fries.

And except that at the end of the day, we drove up the driveway to the farm.

Our dad saw happy memories everywhere he looked. All we could see was old furniture and dust.

Our mom said, "Let's play badminton!"

The racquets were shaped like Potato chips

because they had been left out in the barn for so long.

We played for about one minute, and it started to rain. We ran to the house to wait for the rain to pass over.

But it rained for days.

No one could believe how much it was raining.
Our grandmother said it hadn't rained for weeks.

The television got three channels: the striped channel,
the channel that showed what you could watch if you had
a better TV, and the French channel.

   "Where's the English channel?" my brother asked.

   "Between England and France," said our grandfather.

   Our mother explained how this was a joke.

MY BrotHer
Took THese
Pictures
OF Me.

We thought it might never stop raining. But then it did.

   "Let's go swimming!" said our dad.

He knew about a secret swimming spot. He used to go there all the time with his cousins. We parked the car behind an old apple stand and headed for the secret path.

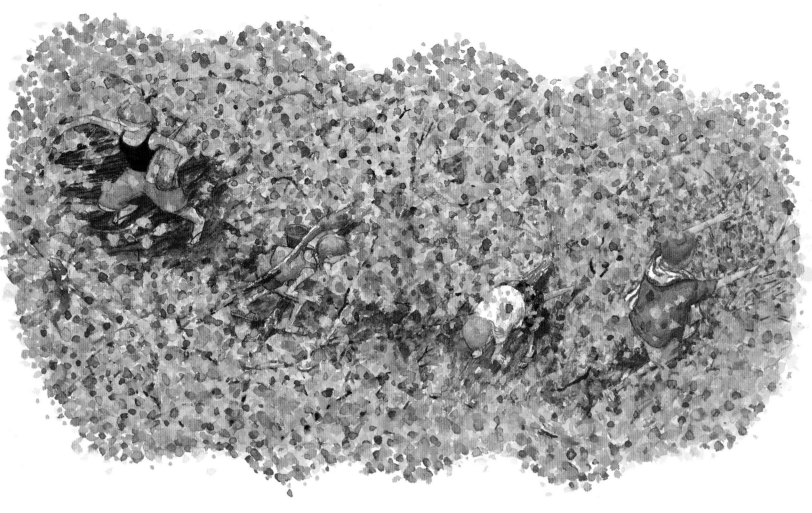

The secret path was even more secret than our dad remembered.

"This was never here before!"
he said. "But don't worry.
It's a big lake. There will be
all kinds of places to swim."

So we hiked back to our car and drove
around looking for one. We drove and
drove but we didn't even see a lake.
Maybe we went the wrong way.

We stopped at a park where there were hills that had been built by people in ancient times. They built them so that from the sky, they looked like a giant sculpture of a serpent. It was a mystery how they did this without being able to see it from the sky. We couldn't see it from the sky, either. From the earth, the hills just looked like hills.

Our mother went off to ask for directions. We watched a squirrel eat noodles from a Chinese food container that someone had left on the ground.

THiS iS a HiLL
Maybe from tHe sky
it LookS Like
a SnaKe.

There was a
Squirrel Here
bat He
ran away.

We got in the car again, but it didn't feel like we would ever get to a lake, or anywhere else.

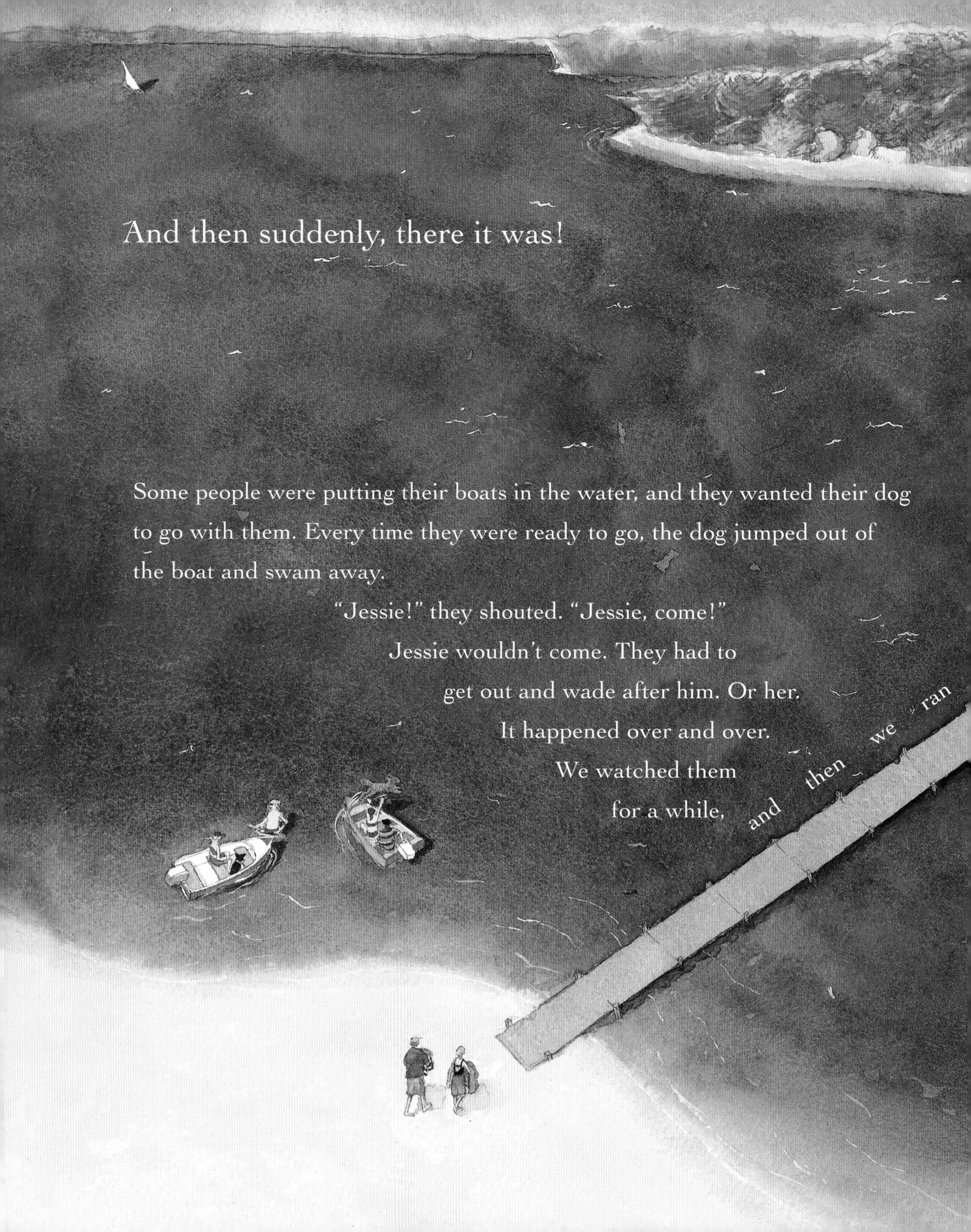

And then suddenly, there it was!

Some people were putting their boats in the water, and they wanted their dog
to go with them. Every time they were ready to go, the dog jumped out of
the boat and swam away.

"Jessie!" they shouted. "Jessie, come!"

Jessie wouldn't come. They had to

get out and wade after him. Or her.

It happened over and over.

We watched them

for a while, and then we ran

all the way out to the end of the dock.

A family was fishing out there,
a mother and a father and a boy.
They smiled and said hi, but then
they spoke in another language.

They seemed excited. We thought they were
telling us about all the fish they were catching.
"That's a lot of fish," we said.
"No," said the boy. He spoke in English.
"They are saying that a storm is coming. Look."
He pointed, and we saw that it was true.

The storm came up so fast that we barely made it to the gazebo in the middle of the dock.

I asked our dad if on our next vacation, we could go someplace like Disney World.

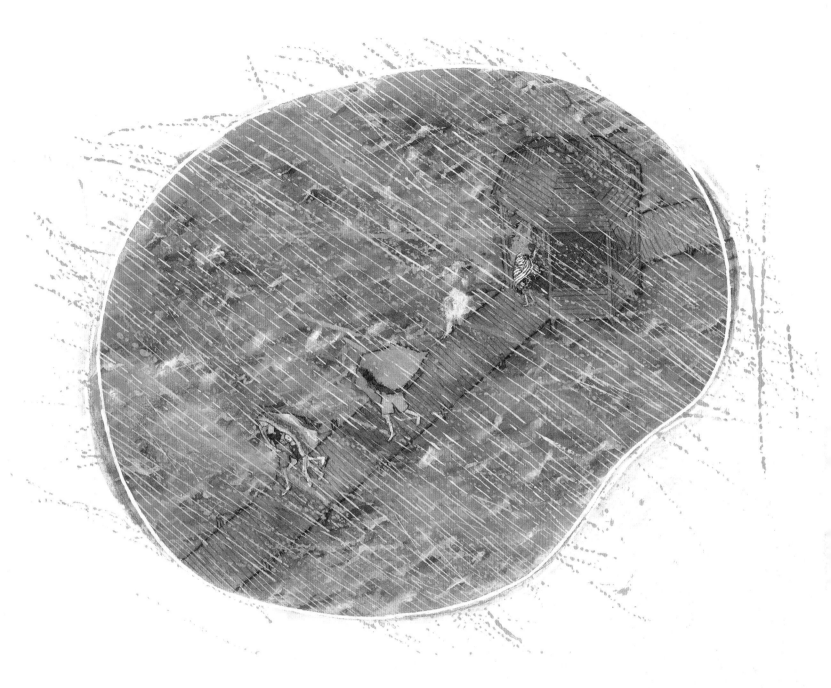

I asked our mom, "Can we do something fun tomorrow?"

   She said, "Well, actually, we have to go to a memorial service."

   "What's a memorial service?" I asked her.

   "It's a kind of church service," she said.

   "Do I have to wear a dress?" I asked.

   "Yes," she said. "You do."

I was thinking that this was turning out to be a stupid vacation, when my brother said that there were cars coming up the driveway. A lot of cars. Voices started to float up through the grate in the floor. Then everyone went to a church, including us.

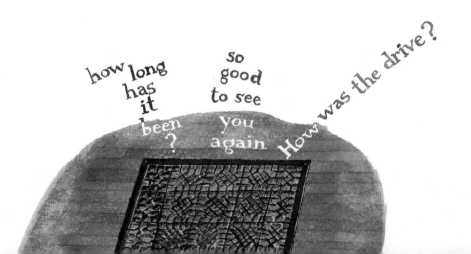

how long has it been?

so good to see you again

How was the drive?

The inside
of the church
was pink.

The church service was about our dad's
Great-aunt Charlotte, who had died a while
ago. She had been old. Everyone still missed
her and they all wanted to tell stories about her.
How when she was young, she learned to fly
an airplane when hardly any women did that.

How once, she chained
herself to a big old tree
that was going to be bulldozed.
And how before she died, she said,
"It's been a long journey."

I whispered to our dad that Aunt Charlotte
sounded interesting. He whispered back
that she was a little bit ornery. "Like you," he said.

It turned out that practically everybody who was there was related to
us somehow—even some people I had never met before. We all went
back to the farm.

We climbed some trees.

Or the next.

Everyone had a story about poison ivy.

Watch out, it's everywhere!

Our cousin found an insect called a walking stick.

At night,
while we were
falling asleep,
some light and
a lot of talking
came up
through the
grate.

Everyone had to leave after a few days, but even when they did,
the old house didn't feel empty the way it had at first.

Then we had to leave, too.

In the car, I took out my notebook and looked at the pictures.

"These don't remind me that much of our vacation," I said.

My brother took out his notebook, too.

"Mine, either," he said.

"You should make sure there's a person in the picture," said our dad. "Pictures are always more interesting if there's a person in them."

"I think you were having too much fun to stop and take pictures," said our mom.

"Maybe we need better cameras," I said.

I looked out the window. There were big electrical towers alongside the highway. I took a picture of them.

In The Picture
They Just Looked Like electric Towers.

In my mind they looked like giant robots marching across the earth, carrying the electricity along in their hands. It's probably hard to take a picture that shows that, even with a really good camera. And it's hard to take a picture of a story someone tells, or what it feels like when you're rolling down a hill or falling asleep in a house full of cousins and uncles and aunts. There are a lot of things like that.

But those kinds of pictures I can keep in my mind.

Only A Star

WRITTEN BY
Margery Facklam
ILLUSTRATED BY
Nancy Carpenter

WILLIAM B. EERDMANS PUBLISHING COMPANY, INC.
Grand Rapids, Michigan • Cambridge, U.K.

Copyright © 1996 Wm. B. Eerdmans Publishing Co.
255 Jefferson Ave., S.E., Grand Rapids, Michigan 49503
P.O. Box 163, Cambridge CB3 9PU U.K.

Printed in Hong Kong

00 99 98 97 96   7 6 5 4 3 2 1

Library of Congress Cataloging-in-Publication Data
Facklam, Margery.
Only a star / by Margery Facklam ; illustrated by Nancy Carpenter.
[32] p. cm. col ill
Summary: A poem describing the star that was present at the first Christmas.
ISBN 0-8028-5122-3
1. Children's poetry, American.   2. Star of Bethlehem— Juvenile poetry.
3. Christmas — Juvenile poetry.   [1. Star of Bethlehem — Poetry.
2. Jesus Christ — Nativity — Poetry. 3. American poetry.]
I. Carpenter, Nancy. ill.   II. Title
JP
FACKLAM   PS3556.A278O54   1996
811'.54— dc20   96-1420
CIP
AC

Designed by Joy Chu

For Katherine Anne Thomas,
who asked the question that became this book.
And in joyful memory of my brother,
David Metz. — M.F.

For Jack and Donna. — N.C.

What were the trimmings
that first Christmas morning?

What brightened the stable
to welcome the Child?
Only a Star.

But it glistened on dewdrops and
turned them to diamonds.
Spidery threads became ribbons of silk.

Even the hay in the hard,
wooden manger
gleamed satin-soft
surrounding the Babe.

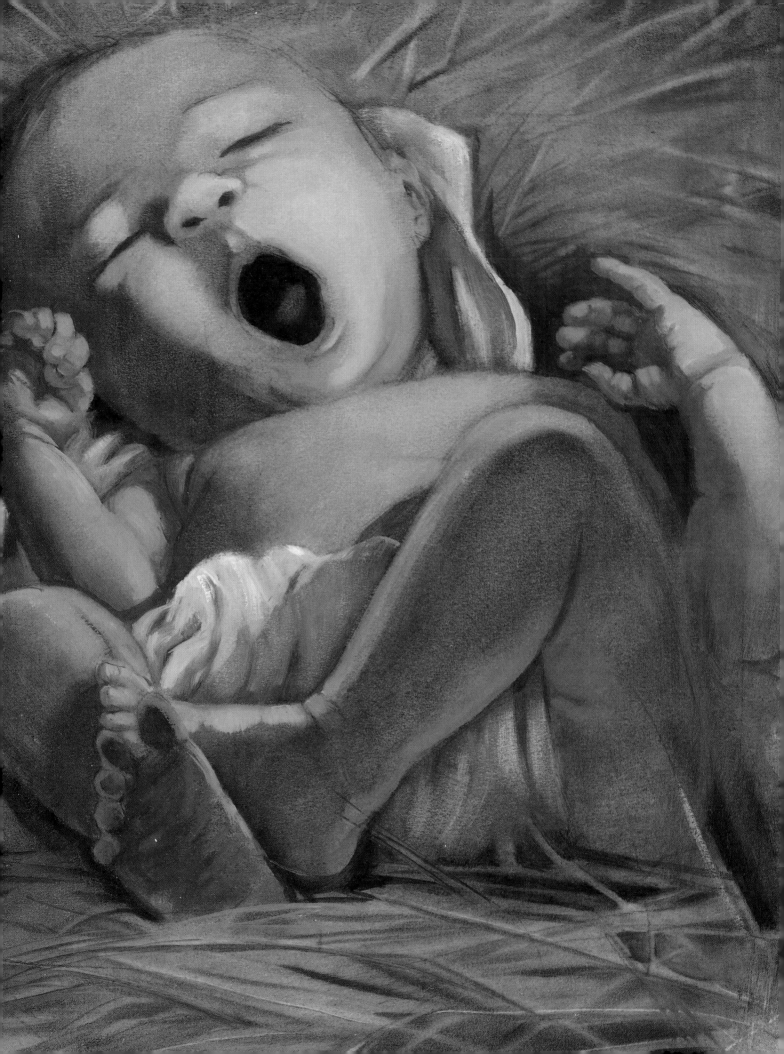

A dragonfly hovered on
wings of clear crystal
scattering the light in a
rainbow of gems.

A scurrying scarab caught in the starglow
added an emerald to trim the Child's bed.

Doves preened
feathers drifted,
like guardian angels
on watch overhead.

Tired from its journey,
a donkey stood silent.
Its worn copper bell glowed
like gold for a King.

Three chubby jerboas danced
in the starlight —
a ritual of joy for this holy day.

A snail left a trail that glittered like tinsel.
Dust sparkled in banners of heavenly light.

Cradled by down in the nest of a nightingale,
eggs became ornaments made for this birth.

What trimmed the stable
that first Christmas morning?

Only a Star,
but it dazzled the earth.

More about the Animals

All the little creatures that brightened the stable in this story lived in the Holy Land when Christ was born, and they live there still.

ORB-WEB SPIDER

More than 3,500 kinds of orb-web spiders spin their silken webs in hidden corners of the world — in gardens, attics, stables, or anywhere they might catch insects. Many people believe it's bad luck to kill a spider or break a web. A book of folklore written in 1866 suggests that this belief began because ". . . when our Blessed Lord lay in the manger, the spider spun a beautiful web, which protected the innocent Babe."

DRAGONFLY

Several different kinds of dragonflies live in the Holy Land. These big insects are carnivores that hunt for other insects during daylight hours, but they might have come awake in the brilliant light of the Christmas Star. In many cultures, the dragonfly is a symbol of renewal and rebirth.

SCARAB BEETLE

All scarab beetles are scavengers that eat dead animals. They are an important part of the world's clean-up crew on every continent except Antarctica. Despite their lowly work, scarab beetles are beautifully colored in shimmery metallic shades of blue, green, purple, bronze, and gold.

DOVE

Long before the birth of Christ, people had begun to domesticate wild rock doves. They raised these birds for food and also trained them to carry messages back to their home roosts. Doves have been symbols of peace, love, and loyalty for thousands of years.

DONKEY

More than 6,000 years ago, small wild donkeys of North Africa were domesticated, and these sturdy, reliable animals have carried people and supplies ever since. At the time of Christ's birth, wealthy people may have owned camels, but it's more likely that Mary rode on a donkey, while Joseph walked beside her as they tried to find a room for the night.

JERBOA

A jerboa is a close cousin to the gerbil. Sometimes it's called a desert rat. As it hops and leaps on its strong hind legs, with its long tail held out for balance, a jerboa looks like a tiny kangaroo. Jerboas stay in their burrows during the heat of the day, but venture out at dusk to look for food. At the Metropolitan Museum of Art in New York City, there is a small sculpture of three jerboas made by an artist about 2,000 years before the birth of Christ. The note on it says: "These tiny creatures inhabit Egypt's desert fringe, where on moonlit nights they can be seen dancing in groups."

SNAIL

Land snails in the Middle East rest during the heat of the day, but when the dew is on the ground at night, they come out to eat plants. Some kinds of land snails stay underground throughout the long, dry summers, and come out only when the ground gets wet with the first autumn rains. But all snails leave a shiny silvery trail behind them as they slide along on their one foot.

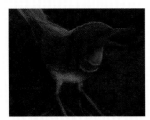

NIGHTINGALE

The nightingale is one of the songbirds mentioned in the Bible. Of all the members of the thrush family, nightingales are most famous for their flutelike, melodious songs. Most birds sing only during the day, but the male nightingale sings his most beautiful songs at night.